THE MELANCHOLY DEATH OF OYSTER BOY & OTHER STORIES

of related interest from Faber and Faber

Burton on Burton

The Art of Sleepy Hollow

THE MELANCHOLY DEATH OF OYSTER BOY & OTHER STORIES

TIM BURTON

FABER & FABER

First published in the United States in 1997
by Rob Weisbach books
An imprint of William Morrow and Company, Inc.
1350 Avenue of the Americas, New York, N.Y. 10019

First published in the United Kingdom in 1998
by Faber and Faber
Bloomsbury House, 74–77 Great Russell Street, London, WC1B 3AU
This paperback edition first published in 2018

Printed in the UK by Bell & Bain Ltd, Glasgow

A CIP record for this book is available from the British Library

ISBN 978–0–571–34510–6

2 4 6 8 10 9 7 5 3 1

for Lisa Marie

Contents

Stick Boy and Match Girl in Love

Stick Boy liked Match Girl,

he liked her a lot.

He liked her cute figure,

he thought she was hot.

But could a flame ever burn

for a match and a stick?

It did quite literally;

he burned up pretty quick.

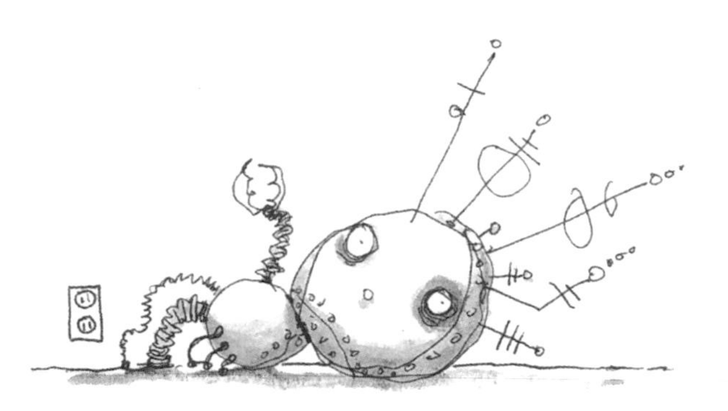

Robot Boy

Mr. and Mrs. Smith had a wonderful life.

They were a normal, happy husband and wife.

One day they got news that made Mr. Smith glad.

Mrs. Smith would be a mom,

which would make him the dad!

But something was wrong with their bundle of joy.

It wasn't human at all,

it was a robot boy!

He wasn't warm and cuddly

and he didn't have skin.

Instead, there was a cold, thin layer of tin.

There were wires and tubes sticking out of his head.

He just lay there and stared,

not living or dead.

The only time he seemed alive at all
was with a long extension cord
plugged into the wall.

Mr. Smith yelled at the doctor,
"What have you done to my boy?
He's not flesh and blood,
he's aluminum alloy!"

The doctor said gently,
"What I'm going to say
will sound pretty wild.
But you're not the father
of this strange-looking child.
You see, there still is some question
about the child's gender,
but we think that its father
is a microwave blender."

The Smiths' lives were now filled

with misery and strife.

Mrs. Smith hated her husband,

and he hated his wife.

He never forgave her unholy alliance:

a sexual encounter

with a kitchen appliance.

And Robot Boy

grew to be a young man.

Though he was often mistaken

for a garbage can.

Staring Girl

I once knew a girl

who would just stand there and stare.

At anyone or anything,

she seemed not to care.

She’d stare at the ground,

She'd stare at the sky.

She'd stare at you for hours,

and you'd never know why.

2
1st
3
1
2
3

But after winning the local staring contest,

she finally gave her eyes

a well-deserved rest.

The Boy with Nails in His Eyes

The Boy with Nails in His Eyes
put up his aluminum tree.
It looked pretty strange
because he couldn't really see.

The Girl with Many Eyes

One day in the park
I had quite a surprise.
I met a girl
who had many eyes.

She was really quite pretty
(and also quite shocking!)
and I noticed she had a mouth,
so we ended up talking.

We talked about flowers,
and her poetry classes,
and the problems she'd have
if she ever wore glasses.

It's great to know a girl
who has so many eyes,
but you really get wet
when she breaks down and cries.

Stain Boy

Of all the super heroes,
the strangest one by far,
doesn't have a special power,
or drive a fancy car.

Next to Superman and Batman,
I guess he must seem tame.
But to me he is quite special,
and Stain Boy is his name.

He can't fly around tall buildings,
or outrun a speeding train,
the only talent he seems to have
is to leave a nasty stain.

Sometimes I know it bothers him,
that he can't run or swim or fly,
and because of this one ability,
his dry cleaning bill's sky-high.

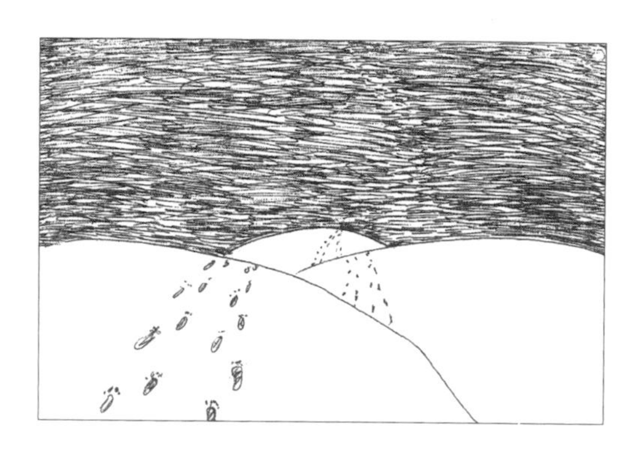

The Melancholy Death of Oyster Boy

He proposed in the dunes,

they were wed by the sea,

their nine-day-long honeymoon

was on the isle of Capri.

For their supper they had one spectacular dish—

a simmering stew of mollusks and fish.

And while he savored the broth,

her bride's heart made a wish.

That wish did come true—she gave birth to a baby.

But was this little one human?

Well,

maybe.

Ten fingers, ten toes,

he had plumbing and sight.

He could hear, he could feel,

but normal?

Not quite.

This unnatural birth, this canker, this blight,

was the start and the end and the sum of their plight.

She railed at the doctor:

"He cannot be mine.

He smells of the ocean, of seaweed and brine."

"You should count yourself lucky, for only last week,

I treated a girl with three ears and a beak.

That your son is half oyster

you cannot blame me.

. . . have you considered, by chance,

a small home by the sea?"

Not knowing what to name him,

they just called him Sam,

or, sometimes,

"that thing that looks like a clam."

Everyone wondered, but no one could tell,

When would young Oyster Boy come out of his shell?

When the Thompson quadruplets espied him one day,

they called him a bivalve and ran quickly away.

One spring afternoon,

Sam was left in the rain.

At the southwestern corner of Seaview and Main,

he watched the rain water as it swirled

down the drain.

His mom on the freeway

in the breakdown lane

was pounding the dashboard—

she couldn't contain

the ever-rising grief,

frustration,

and pain.

"Really, sweetheart," she said,
"I don't mean to make fun,
but something smells fishy
and I think it's our son.
I don't like to say this, but it must be said,
you're blaming our son for your problems in bed."

He tried salves, he tried ointments
that turned everything red.
He tried potions and lotions
and tincture of lead.
He ached and he itched and he twitched and he bled.

The doctor diagnosed,
"I can't be quite sure,
but the cause of the problem may also be the cure.
They say oysters improve your sexual powers.
Perhaps eating your son
would help you do it for hours!"

He came on tiptoe,
he came on the sly,
sweat on his forehead,
and on his lips—a lie.
"Son, are you happy? I don't mean to pry,
but do you dream of Heaven?
Have you wanted to die?"

Sam blinked his eyes twice.

but made no reply.

Dad fingered his knife and loosened his tie.

As he picked up his son,

Sam dripped on his coat.

With the shell to his lips,

Sam slipped down his throat.

Jesus
will
Save

They buried him quickly in the sand by the sea
—sighed a prayer, wept a tear—
and were back home by three.

A cross of gray driftwood marked Oyster Boy's grave.
Words writ in the sand
promised Jesus would save.

But his memory was lost with one high-tide wave.

Back home safe in bed,

he kissed her and said,

"Let's give it a whirl."

"But this time," she whispered, "we'll wish for a girl."

Voodoo Girl

Her skin is white cloth,

and she's all sewn apart

and she has many colored pins

sticking out of her heart.

She has a beautiful set

of hypno-disk eyes,

the ones that she uses

to hypnotize guys.

She has many different zombies

who are deeply in her trance.

She even has a zombie

who was originally from France.

But she knows she has a curse on her,

a curse she cannot win.

For if someone gets

too close to her,

the pins stick farther in.

S

Stain Boy's Special Christmas

For Christmas, Stain Boy got a new uniform.

It was clean and well pressed,

comfy and warm.

But in a few short minutes,

(no longer than ten)

those wet, greasy stains

started forming again.

The Girl Who Turned into a Bed

It happened that day
she picked some strange pussy willow.
Her head swelled up white
and soft as a pillow.

Her skin, which had turned
all flaky and rotten,
was now replaced
with 100% cotton.

Through her organs and torso

she sprouted like wings,

a beautiful set

of mattress and springs.

It was so terribly strange

that I started to weep.

But at least after that

I had a nice place to sleep.

Roy, the Toxic Boy

To those of us who knew him
—his friends—
we called him Roy.
To others he was known
as that horrible Toxic Boy.

He loved ammonia and asbestos,
and lots of cigarette smoke.
What he breathed in for air
would make most people choke!

His very favorite toy
was a can of aerosol spray;
he'd sit quietly and shake it,
and spray it all the day.

He'd stand inside of the garage

in the early-morning frost,

waiting for the car to start

and fill him with exhaust.

The one and only time

I ever saw Toxic Boy cry

was when some sodium chloride

got into his eye.

One day for fresh air

they put him in the garden.

His face went deathly pale

and his body began to harden.

The final gasp of his short life
was sickly with despair.
Whoever thought that you could die
from breathing outdoor air?

As Roy's soul left his body,

we all said a silent prayer.

It drifted up to heaven

and left a hole in the ozone layer.

James

Unwisely, Santa offered a teddy bear to James, unaware that he had been mauled by a grizzly earlier that year.

Stick Boy's Festive Season

Stick Boy noticed that his Christmas tree looked healthier than he did.

Brie Boy

Brie Boy had a dream he only had twice,

that his full, round head was only a slice.

The other children never let Brie Boy play . . .

. . . but at least he went well with a nice Chardonnay.

Mummy Boy

He wasn't soft and pink
with a fat little tummy;
he was hard and hollow,
a little boy mummy.

"Tell us, please, Doctor,
the reason or cause,
why our bundle of joy
is just a bundle of gauze."

"My diagnosis," he said,
"for better or worse,
is that your son is the result
of an old pharaoh's curse."

That night they talked
of their son's odd condition—
they called him "a reject
from an archaeological expedition."

They thought of some complex
scientific explanation,
but assumed it was simple
supernatural reincarnation.

With the other young tots

he only played twice,

an ancient game of virgin sacrifice.

(But the kids ran away, saying, "You aren't very nice.")

Alone and rejected, Mummy Boy wept,

then went to the cabinet

where the snack food was kept.

He wiped his wet sockets with his mummified sleeves,

and sat down to a bowl of sugar-frosted tanna leaves.

One dark, gloomy day,

from out of the fog,

appeared a little white mummy dog.

For his newfound wrapped pet,

he did many things,

like building a dog house

à la Pyramid of Kings.

It was late in the day—

just before dark.

Mummy Boy took his dog

for a walk in the park.

The park was empty

except for a squirrel,

and a birthday party for a Mexican girl.

The boys and girls had all started to play,

but noticed that thing that looked like papier mâché.

"Look, it's a piñata,"

said one of the boys,

"let's crack it wide open

and get the candy and toys."

They took a baseball bat

and whacked open his head.

Mummy Boy fell to the ground;

he finally was dead.

Inside of his head

were no candy or prizes,

just a few stray beetles

of various sizes.

Junk Girl

There once was a girl
who was made up of junk.
She looked really dirty,
and she smelled like a skunk.

She was always unhappy,
or in one of her slumps—perhaps 'cause she spent
so much time down in the dumps.

The only bright moment

was from a guy named Stan.

He was the neighborhood

garbage man.

He loved her a lot

and made a marriage proposal,

but she'd already thrown herself

down a garbage disposal.

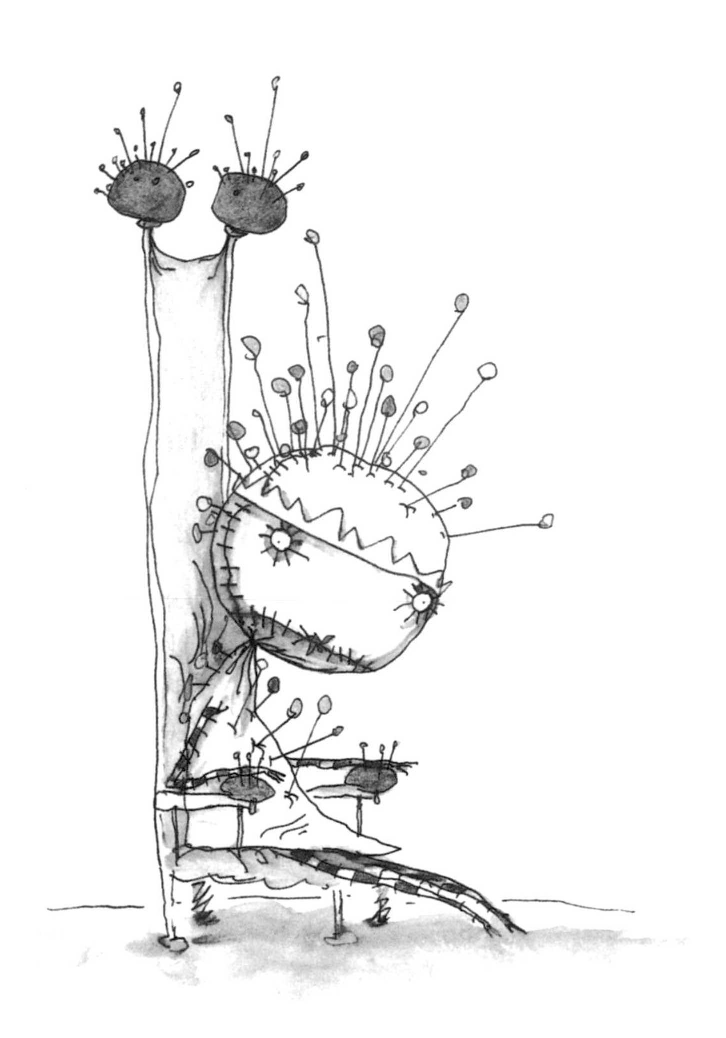

The Pin Cushion Queen

Life isn't easy
for the Pin Cushion Queen.
When she sits on her throne
pins push through her spleen.

Melonhead

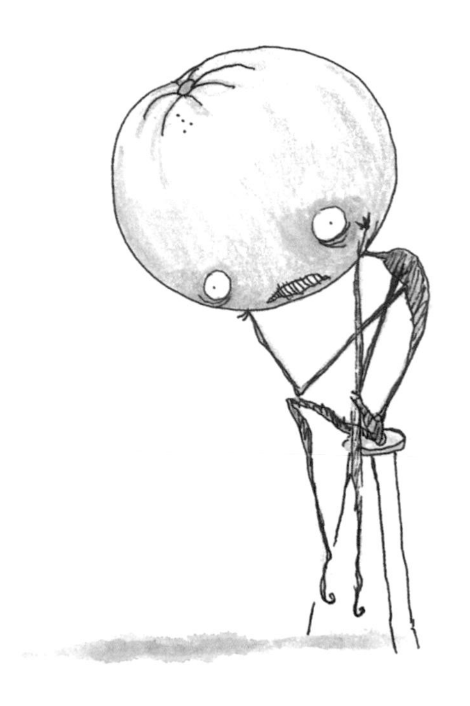

There once was a morose melonhead,

who sat there all day

and wished he were dead.

But you should be careful
about the things that you wish.
Because the last thing he heard
was a deafening squish.

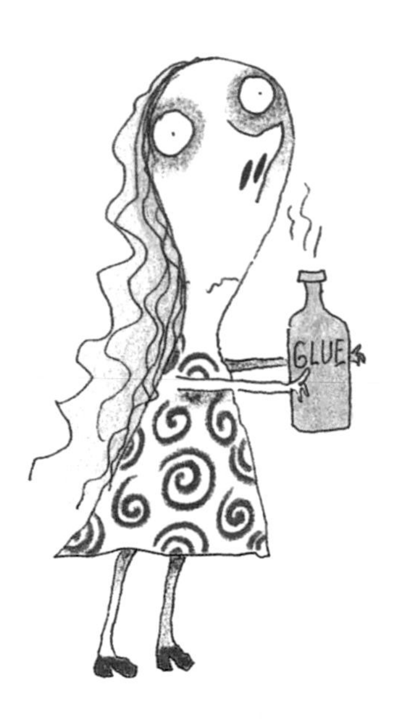
GLUE

Sue

To avoid a lawsuit,

we'll just call her Sue

(or "that girl who likes

to sniff lots of glue").

The reason I know

that this is the case

is when she blows her nose,

kleenex sticks to her face.

Jimmy, the Hideous Penguin Boy

"My name is Jimmy,

but my friends just call me

'the hideous penguin boy.'"

Char Boy

For Christmas, Char Boy received his usual lump of coal,
which made him very happy.

For Christmas, Char Boy received a small present instead of
his usual lump of coal,
which confused him very much.

For Christmas, Char Boy was mistaken for a dirty fireplace
and swept out into the street.

Anchor Baby

There was a beautiful girl
who came from the sea.
And there was just one place
that she wanted to be.

With a man named Walker
who played in a band.
She would leave the ocean
and come onto the land.

He was the one
that she wanted the most.
And she tried everything
to capture this ghost.

But throughout all their lives
they never connected.
She wandered the earth
alone and rejected.

She tried looking happy
she tried looking tragic,
she tried astral projecting,
sex, and black magic.

Nothing could join them,

except maybe one thing,

just maybe . . .

something to anchor their spirits. . . .

They had a baby.

But to give birth to the baby

they needed a crane.

The umbilical cord

was in the form of a chain.

It was ugly and gloomy,

and as hard as a kettle.

It had no pink skin,

just heavy gray metal.

The baby that was meant

to bring them together,

just shrouded them both

in a cloud of foul weather.

So Walker took off

to play with the band.

And from that day on,

he stayed mainly on land.

And she was alone
with her gray baby anchor,
who got so oppressive
that it eventually sank her.

As she went to the bottom,
not fulfilling her wish,
it was her, and her baby . . .
and a few scattered fish.

trick
or
treat

Oyster Boy Steps Out

For Halloween,

Oyster Boy decided to go as a human.

ACKNOWLEDGMENTS

Thanks to Michael McDowell, Jill Jacobs Brack, Rodney Kizziah, Eva Quiroz, and David Szanto.